# HOTEL
# FLAMINGO
## HOLIDAY HEAT WAVE

# Hotel Flamingo

# HOTEL FLAMINGO

## HOLIDAY HEAT WAVE

## ALEX MILWAY

**Kane Miller**

A DIVISION OF EDC PUBLISHING

First American Edition 2020
Kane Miller, A Division of EDC Publishing

Text & Illustrations copyright © Alex Milway 2019
Originally published in the English language as *Hotel Flamingo: Holiday Heatwave* by Piccadilly Press, an imprint of Bonnier Books UK.
The moral rights of the author/illustrator have been asserted.

For information contact:
Kane Miller, A Division of EDC Publishing
P.O. Box 470663
Tulsa, OK 74147-0663
**www.kanemiller.com**
**www.usbornebooksandmore.com**

Library of Congress Control Number: 2019953228

Printed and bound in the United States of America
1 2 3 4 5 6 7 8 9 10
ISBN: 978-1-68464-127-7

*For Gary*

CAN YOU
FIND ME
IN THE STORY?

# 1

# The Royal Letter

In the blazing heat of summer, a long black limousine pulled up outside Hotel Flamingo. The car looked very important, with tiny black, white and orange flags fluttering from its hood. Three smartly dressed penguins stepped out. Two of them played a fanfare on long golden horns – *PAR-RAPPA-PARP!* – as the third waddled over to T. Bear.

This penguin looked incredibly official in a black blazer and pleated skirt, and as she spoke the little round glasses on her beak bobbed up and down.

"I am Ms. Chinstrap, envoy to King Valentin and Queen Julieta Penguin of the Southern Isles," she said, "and I would like to see the owner of Hotel Flamingo."

T. Bear had worked on the door of Hotel Flamingo for what seemed like forever, but he couldn't remember any arrival being quite so extravagant.

"Certainly, Ms. Chinstrap," he said, standing slightly more

upright than before. "Please follow me."

T. Bear ushered the penguin through the lobby, past Lemmy, a wide-eyed ring-tailed lemur on the front desk, and knocked on the office door.

"Ms. Dupont," said T. Bear, pushing the door open, "may I present to you . . . Ms. Chinstrap, envoy to the King and Queen Penguin!"

Anna leapt up from her chair. "Good morning, Ms. Chinstrap," she said nervously. "How can I help?"

Ms. Chinstrap sniffed and gazed around the office, noting every speck of dust, every tilted picture frame and every book out of line on the shelf. "The King and Queen

Penguin would like to stay at your hotel,"
she said.

"Here?" said Anna, a little shocked.
"Really?"

"Yes," said Ms. Chinstrap.

Anna's heart started racing. This
was amazing news, but she'd never met
royalty before. Her thoughts ran away
with themselves. How do you cook for
a king or queen? Do they talk the same
language as everyone else?

"And . . . er . . . when are our royal
guests hoping to stay?" she asked.

"In three days' time, and staying for
seven nights," said Ms. Chinstrap. "They
apologize for their last-minute decision.
The Queen decided she would like to try
something different from the Glitz."

The Glitz was an exclusive hotel and Hotel Flamingo's main competition on Animal Boulevard. Its owner, Mr. Ruffian, did everything in his power to make life difficult for Anna.

"They chose us over the Glitz?" said Anna, astonished.

"Please be aware that if Hotel Flamingo falls below the standards necessary," said Ms. Chinstrap, "it is perfectly easy to return there."

"Standards?"

Ms. Chinstrap removed a black folder from her handbag and passed it to Anna.

"You'll find all the information you need in here," she said, tapping the folder with her wing. "Inside is a list of all royal requirements, from meals to room decoration."

Anna flipped through the folder, scanning page after page of instructions. "Good grief, there's a lot, isn't there?" she said.

Ms. Chinstrap dipped her head and squawked. "As royal envoy," she said, "I have a duty to ensure that everything is perfect. Perfection is my name, my aim and my absolute game."

"Oh, mine too!" said Anna. "I love perfection."

Ms. Chinstrap raised a feathery eyebrow above her glasses and leaned across to correct Anna's slanting hat. "We're facing a heat wave, and penguins are not suited to extreme heat. I take it you will be able to deal with that?"

"Of course," said Anna. "You'll need ice, and lots of it."

"That would be a good start," said Ms. Chinstrap. "I will return for a full tour of the hotel tomorrow, but now I will leave you to prepare. Remember, Ms. Dupont, royalty deserves perfection!" And with that she waddled out of the office.

Anna gulped as the news sank in. A real-life king and queen were coming to Hotel Flamingo. She had to tell everyone!

"STOP EVERYTHING!" she cried, circling the lobby with her hands waving above her head. "STAFF MEETING! MY OFFICE! NOW!"

T. Bear gathered everyone together. Stella Giraffe stood head and shoulders above everybody, with Madame Le Pig,

Eva Koala, Lemmy, Squeak the mouse and Hilary Hippo wondering what all the fuss was about.

"The King and Queen Penguin are coming to stay!" cried Anna, excitedly.

Everyone gasped and Eva Koala clapped with joy.

"But the Royal Suite's not been used for years!" said Lemmy. "Not since Queen Bee moved in with her family of a thousand and sixty-three."

"The honey was amazing," said T. Bear blissfully.

Hilary Hippo sneezed at the very thought of how dirty the room might be.

"There's much to do," Anna said, "but a royal visit will really put us on the Animal Boulevard map! Everyone, to work!"

# 2
# New Guests

Even without preparations for a
royal visit Hotel Flamingo was
busier than ever before. It was
the height of summer, and as old
guests departed new ones arrived.
Just when the midday sun was
reaching its hottest, and Lemmy
was wishing he could take a
siesta, a tour bus arrived.

Along with a large party of grumpy warthogs and giggly meerkats, there were three monkeys and a family of zebras – not to mention a strangely colored lizard and a lone rat in a bright-red dress. They surged through the revolving doors and into the lobby.

"Welcome to our hotel!" announced Anna, ushering everyone inside.

Every creature had differing needs, and Anna could see that there would be a lot to get right and an awful lot that could go wrong with this new busload of guests.

Luckily Lemmy was on hand to help. He noticed that the rat had more luggage than most creatures twice her size and was trapped among a gaggle of meerkats, who were laughing and bantering with

each other. He checked
his books for her name.

"Ms. Ronnie
Rathbone?" asked
Lemmy, waving to
catch her attention.

"That's me," she
replied. She danced
through the crowd
smiling, two gold teeth glistening in her
mouth.

Lemmy handed over her room key.
"You're in 512, miss," he said, leaving the
desk to help with her bags. He struggled
to pick them up. "Wow! What's in there?"

"I always take everything wherever I
go," said Ronnie. "Just in case."

"Just in case what?" asked Lemmy.

"I'm a rat," said Ronnie. "Always getting kicked out of places. Always being moved on."

"Rest assured, Hotel Flamingo welcomes everyone!" said Lemmy.

"I'm pleased to hear it," said Ronnie.

Lemmy dragged the luggage into the elevator. "Have a good stay, miss."

Ronnie winked. "I will, kid. I always do."

Before he could return to his desk, a frowning warthog approached with two wriggling hoglets in each arm.

"Excuse me," she said with a snort.

"Ah yes," he said. "Your name?"

"Mrs. Bamba. I'm the head of the warthog party," she replied.

Lemmy picked up the keys to all their

16

rooms. "Any special requirements for your stay?" he asked.

"Mud for our baths," said Mrs. Bamba. "That's about all."

"I thought baths got you clean, not dirty?" asked Lemmy.

"No, no. You've got it all wrong," said Mrs. Bamba. She placed her troublesome hoglets down and they rolled off in a blur of trotters. "Smearing mud on our bristles keeps us looking young. You should try it!"

Lemmy patted his face, wondering if he was looking old.

"Enough for all twenty-six of us warthogs," added Mrs. Bamba.

Lemmy quickly did the math. That was a lot of mud. "I'll do my best," he said.

"Just simple clean mud, please," said Mrs. Bamba. "No fancy smells."

She stomped off, leaving Lemmy wondering where to find a wheelbarrow and some simple clean mud. It would be easier said than done.

Anna took care of the lizard while Lemmy dealt with the rest of the guests. She was so mesmerized by his bright-green and red skin that she almost forgot her manners. "I'm sorry," she said, realizing that she had been staring. "Mr. Camou?"

The lizard tugged at his collar with spindly yet precise fingers and placed his

expensive hand luggage on the front desk. "It is no problem," he said proudly, with a slow nod. "I know I look wonderful. If I was you, I'd stare at me all the time."

Anna forced a smile as she handed over a key. "Room 102. I hope you enjoy your stay."

The lizard took out his mobile phone to make a call, before tiptoeing away across the lobby. Once the zebras, monkeys and meerkats had been cared for, Anna returned to the front desk.

"We've got our work cut out this week," said Lemmy. "A royal visit is the last thing we need."

"Just keep doing what you do so well, Lemmy," said Anna. "All will be well."

But Lemmy knew better. "Just you

wait," he said. "The king and queen will have you running in circles before they've even stepped through the door."

"Oh, it can't be that bad," said Anna. "Besides, we *are* a hotel! Looking after people is what we do."

"You're right, miss, of course," said Lemmy.

Anna patted him on the back. "That's the spirit!" she said.

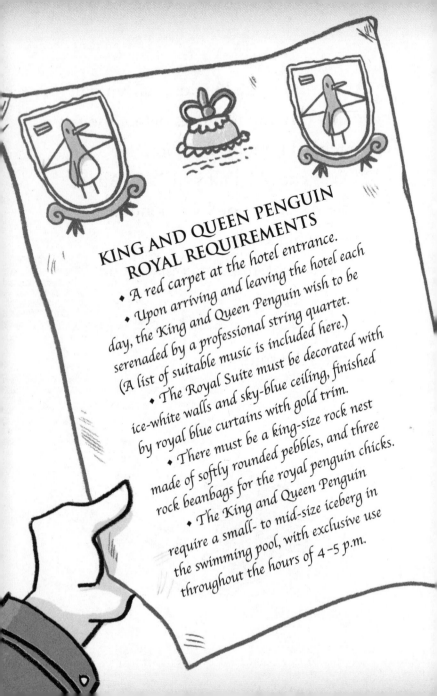

# KING AND QUEEN PENGUIN ROYAL REQUIREMENTS

- A red carpet at the hotel entrance.
- Upon arriving and leaving the hotel each day, the King and Queen Penguin wish to be serenaded by a professional string quartet. (A list of suitable music is included here.)
- The Royal Suite must be decorated with ice-white walls and sky-blue ceiling, finished by royal blue curtains with gold trim.
- There must be a king-size rock nest made of softly rounded pebbles, and three rock beanbags for the royal penguin chicks.
- The King and Queen Penguin require a small- to mid-size iceberg in the swimming pool, with exclusive use throughout the hours of 4–5 p.m.

# Perfection is Everything

The following morning, as promised, Ms. Chinstrap arrived for a tour of the hotel. Anna had spent many hours reading the list of royal requirements, and it had only made her nerves worse.

They took the elevator up as far as it could go, then stepped out into a beautifully decorated hallway.

ceci n'est pas une pig

"The Royal Suite!" said Anna, folder in hand. She prepared for the worst as they walked inside.

The Royal Suite occupied the entire top floor of the hotel, and Anna was relieved to see Hilary had cleaned the rooms to perfection as always. They looked old and faded, but the suite was definitely grand and worthy of a king or queen.

The penguin waddled in and checked every detail with the beady eyes of someone who had done this many times before.

"What do you think?" asked Anna.

Ms. Chinstrap hummed and hawed. "This wall color does nothing for me except give me a headache," she said. "In fact, I may vomit."

"Please don't – we've just cleaned the carpets," said Anna.

She received a stern look from Ms. Chinstrap, and Anna realized this probably wasn't the time for jokes.

"The correct royal color is noted in the folder," said Ms. Chinstrap. "Do change it."

"Paint it?" Anna replied.

"Of course," said the penguin. "The fresh colors calm the king and queen when in faraway places."

"Yes, marm," said Anna.

"Oh no, no, no. I am not the queen!" said the penguin. "And it is 'ma'am' as in 'jam.' Follow the details on how to address royalty in your folder. Perfection, after all, is –"

"Everything," finished Anna.

She was starting to understand the enormity of the task that lay ahead. There were so many things to remember and get right. But Anna was determined to do just that.

"And these curtains are not suitable," said the penguin, running her wing down their length. "And I can see from here the beds are far too soft. Penguins like rocks, not mattresses. I could go on, but it's all in the royal requirements . . ."

"Yes, marm," said Anna, "I mean,
ma'am, I mean, Ms. Chinstrap."

Ms. Chinstrap rattled her head and
stared at Anna with a beady eye. "Now
I should like to meet the chef," she said.

Anna gulped. "Right," she said.
"Follow me."

# 4

# Ruffled Feathers

Madame Le Pig was knee-deep in a giant saucepan of berries when Anna reached the kitchen and opened the door. "Sorry to interrupt, chef," she said.

"How dare you disrupt *le chef* when she is squishing fruit!" squealed Madame Le Pig. "It is a very private moment!"

Anna coughed to alert the chef to the important person standing beside her.

"I wanted to introduce you to the royal envoy," she said, "Ms. Chinstrap."

Madame Le Pig turned, frowned and pulled her bright-purple, berry-stained trotters from the pan. She cleaned them on a tea towel. "Ach. This is most inconvenient!" she said.

"We have heard great things of your skill, Madame Le Pig," said Ms. Chinstrap.

"Of course you have," the chef replied. "That is because I am the best in the land. Good enough for any king or queen!"

"The king and queen have prepared their own menu for you," said the envoy.

"WHAT?" screamed the chef.

Ms. Chinstrap took the folder from Anna and removed a list.

**Breakfast:** a platter of krill marmalade on triangular-cut toast.

**Lunch:** crispy samphire tempura with iceberg lettuce garnish.

**Tea:** squid scones and fishcakes with clotted cream and seaweed jam.

**Supper:** steamed fish on a bed of freshly cut seaweed.

**Dessert:** sea slug meringue.

"Please take time to perfect and prepare these meals," said Ms. Chinstrap. "I will be official taster to Their Majesties, and will approve each course. Perfection is what we're after."

"PERFECTION!" exploded Madame Le Pig. "I am the most perfect chef on Animal Boulevard. I am so perfect I could throw a wooden spoon from the other side of the kitchen and I know it would hit you perfectly on the beak!"

Anna leapt in to cool the situation. "All will be well!" she said, forcing a smile. "Won't it, chef?"

Madame Le Pig stared at the list of meals, almost burning holes into the paper with her eyes. "I do not like or make squid scones," she spat.

"They are the queen's favorite," said Ms. Chinstrap. "It is very important she has them."

"Surely squid scones cooked by you would be the best squid scones on Animal Boulevard?" said Anna to Madame Le Pig. She was getting much better at handling the chef these days.

"That is correct!" said Madame Le Pig.

"Then I think you should allow the queen to try them," Anna replied.

The pig mulled it over for a second. "I agree," she said. "The queen deserves to eat my squid scones."

Anna showed Ms. Chinstrap out into the restaurant. "I assure you, she is the best in the land," she said.

"Oh, she is precisely everything I

expected of a top-class chef," said the penguin.

After a brief tour around the rest of the hotel, Ms. Chinstrap declared it was time to leave. "I look forward to our stay," she said, approaching T. Bear and the revolving doors. "Remember: to upset royalty is to face ruin! I am a true perfectionist, and, as you know –"

"Perfection is everything," finished Anna.

As the penguin drove off down Animal Boulevard, Anna's shoulders slumped.

"You all right, miss?" asked T. Bear.

"What have I gotten us into, Mr. Bear?" she said.

"Oh, don't worry, miss," said T. Bear, smiling. "We've had more difficult guests than penguins. You should have been here when the Komodo dragon stayed! We had to keep a really close watch on that one, I can tell you."

A procession of young, muddy hoglets ran through the lobby, leaving dirty footprints everywhere. T. Bear looked sad. "I'll get the dustpan and brush," he grumbled.

# 5

# Mr. Ruffian

Anna was working through her list of jobs when the bell at the front desk chimed impatiently over and over again.

"DOES NO ONE WORK HERE ANYMORE?" roared a voice.

Anna recognized it immediately and feared the worst. The voice belonged to Mr. Ronald Ruffian, the lion owner of the Glitz Hotel.

Mr. Ruffian roared in anger as Anna approached. He was waving a letter written on silver paper. "The King and Queen Penguin were supposed to be staying at my hotel, but now they've canceled!" he said.

"Yes, because they're coming here instead," said Anna proudly.

"Royalty always stays at the Glitz," snarled Mr. Ruffian.

"Not anymore," said Anna.

"You're making a big mistake, taking my business," growled Mr. Ruffian, pointing a manicured claw at Anna.

"Mark my words, this is the biggest –
THE ABSOLUTE BIGGEST – mistake
you've ever made. I will make their stay
impossible for you, if it's
the last thing I do."

Then Mr. Ruffian
flicked back his mane
and stomped out of
the hotel, bumping
T. Bear aside
on the way.

"I don't like the sound of that," said
Lemmy, arriving in the lobby pushing a
wheelbarrow full of mud.

"Nor me," said Anna. She looked at
Lemmy's wheelbarrow with confusion.

"Don't worry," he said, forcing a smile.
"Everything's under control."

"Do you want to tell me something, Lemmy?" asked Anna.

"No! You have enough to worry about."

"Good," she said. "Don't suppose you know where I might find an iceberg in the height of summer? The penguins need it for the swimming pool."

Lemmy lowered the wheelbarrow to the floor and scratched his ear. "You could try the port," he said. "Back in the day that's where we got our ice from. They used to ship it across the sea on big boats."

"I'd forgotten that," said T. Bear. "It's worth a try."

"I'll do just that then," said Anna.

She gave T. Bear the list, before collecting her sun hat. "Can you ask Stella to redecorate the Royal Suite?" she said. "And we really need a red carpet."

"Don't you worry, miss," said T. Bear, waving the list confidently. "We definitely have one somewhere."

Anna was relieved. "Then I'm off to find an iceberg!" she said.

•

Lemmy trundled the wheelbarrow into the elevator, passing Mrs. Turpington the very old tortoise. She lived in the hotel and was always late for breakfast.

"Morning, young Lemmy," she said. "Or is it afternoon?"

"Afternoon," said Lemmy, smiling.

"Ah," she said, chuckling. "I hope there's still some lettuce soup left for me!"

"I'm sure there will be, Mrs. Turpington," he replied.

Lemmy traveled upward to the fourth floor and knocked on Mrs. Bamba's door. "Mud delivery!" he called.

The door opened and three hoglets

raced out, sniffing and snorting and bouncing off the walls.

"Perfect!" said Mrs. Bamba. Her head was wrapped up in a towel. "I've just had a shower, but it's really not the same without mud."

Lemmy smiled and pushed the wheelbarrow into the room.

"How much do you need?" he asked.

"All of it," said Mrs. Bamba.

Lemmy looked at his pile of mud with a sense of crushing sadness. He'd hoped he'd dug up enough for all the warthogs.

"OK then," he said, tipping his wheelbarrow into the bath. "I'll be back soon with the rest."

# 6

# The Port

Anna left the taxi and approached the quayside. Animal Boulevard faced the sea and its port was always busy. Towering cargo ships overshadowed stylish cruise liners, which looked down on tiny fishing boats bobbing on the waves.

A welcome breeze almost lifted off Anna's hat as she pushed through crowds of tourists toward a muscle-bound tiger who was directing the movement of crates and containers.

"Hello," said Anna to the tiger. "Have there been any shiploads of ice this morning?"

"At this time of the day?" he said, laughing. "You've got to get up right early to grab ice round 'ere. With this hot weather everyone's after it!"

"So no chance of an iceberg then?"

The tiger almost collapsed with laughter.

"Nah, mate, you've got more chance of buying a dinosaur," he said.

*The King and Queen Penguin will not be happy*, thought Anna.

The tiger lifted his sunglasses to offer up a secret. "I tell you what – and I shouldn't really be tellin' you this," he said, pointing his paw at Anna, "but the last load that came in was snapped up by that Glitz hotel. They bought up enough ice to fill a swimming pool."

"Did they now," grumbled Anna.

"You could try asking them for some?" said the tiger.

"I don't think they'd help me," she replied. "But thank you."

Anna slouched all the way home. She suspected Mr. Ruffian had bought up all of the ice on purpose. What would he do next?

•

Anna spent the rest of the afternoon on the telephone, asking everyone and anyone for help. Every curtain maker was busy, every rock shop was sold out, every string quartet was booked up, and there was absolutely no ice to be found. Mr. Ruffian had bought up everything! She started to think she might never get the hotel ready in time when there came a knock at the door.

"Miss Anna," said Hilary Hippo, "might I come in?"

"Please do," said Anna.

"I may have accidentally overheard a few things while dusting outside," said Hilary. "Might I be so bold as to suggest we solve these royal problems ourselves?"

"What do you mean?" asked Anna.

"I could make the curtains for you," said Hilary. "I'm sure there's everything we need here in the hotel."

Anna's spirits suddenly lifted. "You really mean it?"

"Cleaning is not my only skill," said Hilary. "I've got three degrees. I've been a bank manager and a football coach, and I once taught sewing at the Savannah School of Stitching."

"Wow!" said Anna. "I never knew. If only you'd been to music school as well! Finding a string quartet is proving a real problem."

"Surely you must know *someone* musical?" asked Hilary.

Anna thought and thought and thought some more. And then the answer presented itself.

"Good grief," said Anna. "I *do* know someone musical. Ms. Fragranti!"

"The flamingo?" said Hilary.

Anna skipped around her office, suddenly feeling as though the tide was turning.

"Yes!" cried Anna. "Her school of flamingos can do anything! Magic, theater, dance. They are sure to play instruments too! I'll call her straightaway. Mr. Ruffian will not get the better of us!"

Hilary shook her feather duster in excitement and sneezed so hard she blew Anna's hat off. "Sorry," she said. "I don't know the strength of my own nose."

# 7

# Carpet Troubles

T. Bear found the hotel's red carpet rolled
up in a wooden storage shed on the
garden terrace. The felted roof had long
been in need of repair, and everything
inside was damp. T. Bear lifted the
carpet onto his shoulder and blanched.

"Pooh!" said Lemmy, trundling past
with another wheelbarrow of mud.
"What's that?"

"The red carpet," said T. Bear.

"It stinks," said Lemmy, hurrying on. "No one will want to tread on that!"

"I'd better find Hilary and clean it then," T. Bear said gruffly.

"Excuse me," said Mr. Camou, tapping him on the shoulder.

T. Bear was startled to find the lizard beside the shed. He was sure he hadn't been there a second ago, but maybe he had just been too preoccupied with the awful smell of the carpet to notice him. "Yes, sir?"

"It's so hot out here," said Mr. Camou, "and I am so worried about my beautiful skin. Might you have some sunblock I could borrow?"

"I keep it at the front desk," said T. Bear. "You should ask there."

"Marvelous," said the lizard. "Cheerio!"

T. Bear searched the hotel top and bottom for Hilary. He even started asking guests if they'd seen her, which was terribly unprofessional. Only Ronnie Rathbone offered any help, and on her directions he eventually found the hippo nose-deep in a storage cupboard, searching for material.

"Have you got anything to freshen this up?" asked T. Bear, presenting the carpet.

Hilary sniffed it and turned up her very large nose. "There are two different soap powders in my cleaning cupboard," she said. "One is weak for use on everything, and the other is superstrong to clean between my toes only. Be sure to use the right one!"

T. Bear looked worried. "How will I know which is the right one?" he asked.

"Green for weak, red for superstrong," she said.

"Right," growled T. Bear.

"Now, remember, shake it on, then

vacuum it off. And, above all, do not add water."

"Yes," growled T. Bear. He never knew cleaning could be so complicated.

# 8

## To the Rescue

Anna was not one to waste time. An iceberg was always going to be difficult to find, but perhaps rocks would be easier. So she smeared sunscreen on her face, grabbed an empty bag and marched out of the hotel toward the sea.

The coastal path ran along the cliffs and beaches that surrounded Animal Boulevard, and where there were cliffs there were rocks. Anna loved hunting for shells, and this was no different. She just needed to find a selection of softly rounded pebbles fit for the King and Queen Penguin's bottoms – as well as some for the royal chicks. *I can always put the stones back later,* she thought.

Savannah Beach was the closest beach to the hotel, and its vast swathe of bright sand was rippling in the heat and heaving with sun-loving animals. Lizards big and small stretched out, charging themselves with the sun's rays, and young monkeys hurtled back and forth into the sea's foaming surf.

Anna meandered through the towels and deck chairs to where the golden sands butted up against tall gray cliffs.

There were rocks
everywhere, some smooth,
some jagged.

She began her search, but before her
bag was full, a scream rang out from the
water's edge.

"SHARK!" shouted a young seal, who
had been lazing on a surfboard.

Anna looked up and spotted a fin
rising out of the water close to the shore.
It was curled and tired looking.

It disappeared under the water and surfaced again a few yards farther away.

"That doesn't look like a shark," said Anna, running toward the sea.

"Get away from the water!" cried an elephant lifeguard, urging Anna away. "It's dangerous!"

"It's not a shark!" shouted Anna.

She took off her shoes and socks, dropped her bag on the sand and waded into the water.

The lifeguard waved furiously. But Anna pushed herself farther through the cool water until she was just a few feet from the fin.

"It's a young blue whale!" cried Anna. "And it needs help!"

The lifeguard's ears flapped open, and her trunk blew out a clarion call.

The elephant stormed up the beach and bounced into the water, soaking Anna from head to toe.

"I should have known better," said the elephant, forcing her trunk under the whale to lift it from the water.

Anna spotted the lifeguard's name badge. Her name was Liza.

"Liza," said Anna, "this whale is exhausted. We have to get him back out to deeper waters and his parents."

"I'm on it," said Liza, calling for help on her radio.

As Anna stroked the whale's head he opened his eyes. "Ohhh, Mum will be really mad," he whimpered. "I thought I was strong enough to go for a swim on my own, but the tide was too much."

"I'm sure your mum will just be pleased to see you again," Anna replied with a smile. "Where are you staying?"

"At Holiday Bay," said the whale. "We'd only just arrived."

Anna was pleased to see a lifeboat powering around the coast toward them.

"Fancy a ride?" said Liza.

"You bet!" Anna cried.

And before she knew it, Anna was strapped into the speedboat, bouncing over the waves, comforting the tired blue whale as they hurried back to its parents.

They reached Holiday Bay and its clusters of floating thatched shelters.

A pod of blue whales swam over to them, spraying fountains of water into the air. They rolled and dipped, breaking the water in joy. The largest whale, easily three times the size of the lifeboat, pushed her head from the water to thank Anna and the elephant for returning her son.

"Oh, my watery eyes! Young Podly has returned!" she said. "We'd just arrived from Antarctica and he was determined to go for a swim. I thought I'd lost him forever!"

"Well, you have Anna to thank for rescuing him," said Liza.

"If there's anything I can do to repay you, please tell me," said the whale. "Absolutely anything."

Anna thought for a moment. "Did you mention Antarctica?" She had heard of the place, and knew it was colder than cold and full of ice.

"That's right," said the whale.

"I don't suppose you'd know where to find a small iceberg?" she asked. "I'm in need of one at Hotel Flamingo."

"We passed thousands of them on the way here!" said the whale, squirting water into the air. "I could have one here by tomorrow."

"Do you mean it?" said Anna, with a cheer.

The whale broke the water and slammed onto her side. "I will bring you the best, bluest iceberg you ever saw," she said.

# 9

# Flamingos for Hire

The day before the king and queen were due to arrive, Anna took in a delivery of flowers and proceeded to display them in the lobby. She wanted to make everything look perfect!

"I can't believe we've beaten Mr. Ruffian," she said, squeezing a large bunch of daisies into a very small vase. "Everything Ms. Chinstrap wanted, we've got."

"Probably best to wait and see," said Lemmy, who was wiser than he looked. He took a handful of dahlias and fanned them out. "They're already starting to droop," he said, annoyed.

"You'll need to keep them watered," said Ronnie Rathbone. She took a sip of an iced coffee.

"It's so frustrating," said Anna. "I have enough to deal with already."

"That's heat waves for you," said Ronnie. "Still, I like the heat." She danced away, snatching a flower and threading it behind her ear as she went.

"Why is it so hot?" asked Anna.

"I saw it on the news," said Lemmy. "We're having a serious heat wave, and it's only going to get hotter."

"It's a good thing we have air-conditioning then," said Anna. "Can you make sure it's turned up full blast?"

"You bet," said Lemmy.

As he set off, the revolving doors spun and a flash of bright pink caught Anna's attention. The flamingos had arrived!

"You called, and we came, darling!" cried Ms. Fragranti. "So lovely to be back."

Mrs. Fragranti and her dancing flamingos had helped to save Hotel Flamingo once before. Now Anna was hoping they'd do it again. "I'm so glad you're here!" she said, hugging her friend. "I don't know what I'd do without you."

T. Bear bundled in through the door, struggling to get a large cello case inside.

Ms. Fragranti frowned. "Be careful, Mr. Bear."

"Don't worry," he grumbled. "It's all under control."

"It looks quite the opposite," said Ms. Fragranti.

Four brightly dressed flamingos followed T. Bear inside, suitcases and instruments tucked under their wings.

"Meet our supergroup!" said Ms. Fragranti, ushering her classical music students inside. "This is Tutti, Dolce, Largo and Fermata. All wonderful players. All looking forward to playing for royalty!"

"The king and queen arrive tomorrow," said Anna. "We're trying to get everything ready, but it's been a bit of a battle."

"It's all looking wonderful, darling!"
exclaimed Ms. Fragranti. "But then, it
could never look any different!"

Anna loved having Ms. Fragranti in
the hotel. She was always so supportive
and positive about everything. *When in
doubt, ask a flamingo for help*, she thought.

•

Later that day, as guests were taking their seats in the restaurant for dinner, Anna heard a loud trumpet from the terrace. She raced out to find Jojo the sea otter watching Liza and two other elephant lifeguards pushing a giant blue iceberg up and over the sand dunes.

"That's not something you see every day," said Jojo.

"This big enough for you?" shouted Liza.

It was. *Not even a heat wave will melt that iceberg any time soon*, thought Anna.

"It's perfect!" she cried.

The elephants hauled the iceberg over the terrace. Then, with a loud sploshy clunk, it slipped into the pool. Gallons of water coursed over the poolside, narrowly missing Mr. Camou, who was lounging on a deck chair.

SPLOSH!

"Swimming laps is going to be tricky now," said Jojo, scratching her head.

"It's what the penguins wanted," said Anna with a shrug.

"What about our other guests, though?"

"They're going to love it!" said Anna.

# 10

# Last-Minute Preparations

On the day of the royal visit, alarm clocks
were set extra early so that everything
would be ready. Lemmy was working
the front desk with bigger bags than
usual under his eyes. Having hung her
new curtains, Hilary was engaged in a
final spot of dusting, and Eva was tidying
the restaurant after a particularly messy
breakfast. No matter how fine the dining,

warthogs were
determined to eat
out of troughs!
Outside the hotel,
it was now so hot that
everyone was doing
their best to keep out of
the sun – or cool themselves
down. Stella Giraffe had a
long hose wrapped around her
shoulders and was watering
the hanging baskets, making
sure she sprayed water
over herself at every
opportunity. Even T. Bear
had smeared his fur with
white sunscreen to

stop himself
getting burnt.

"You look more like
a polar bear," said Stella, laughing.

"Actually, my great-aunt *was* a polar
bear," T. Bear revealed, unfurling his
freshly cleaned red carpet along the
pavement. "How does this look?"

"It's scrubbed up well," replied Stella.

The revolving door spun and Ronnie
Rathbone stepped out onto the red
carpet.

T. Bear leapt to his feet. "Sorry, miss!"
he said, frantically shooing her away.
"This carpet is for royalty only."

"I thought everyone was welcome
here?" said Ronnie with a huff. "No
special treatment, you know?"

"Of course everyone's welcome here, miss," said T. Bear, "but this carpet has been cleaned especially for the King and Queen Penguin."

"Suit yourself," sniffed Ronnie, stepping away. She pulled her handbag up over her shoulder and walked a short distance down the pavement before stopping. Something had caught her attention.

"Is that cheering?" said T. Bear. "Could it be —"

"It's them all right," said Stella. "The royals." She wiped her hooves on her overalls and turned off the hose.

"I'd better go and clean myself up!"

A shiver ran down T. Bear's spine as he spotted the procession of black cars heading very slowly down Animal Boulevard.
The cars were trailed by a giddy pack of photographers and well-wishers.

T. Bear ran off to tell everyone, and as he did Ronnie skipped gleefully back along the red carpet.

# 11

# The King and Queen Penguin

Three limousines with tiny flags flying from their hoods drew to a stop outside Hotel Flamingo. Every member of staff lined up beside the red carpet to welcome the royals.

Anna straightened her hat. "Here we go," she said under her breath.

A door clicked open on the first limousine. Two royal heralds, dressed in top hats and tails despite the heat, stepped out and raised their trumpets. They played a bold fanfare as a second group of footpenguins, led by Ms. Chinstrap, left the cars and opened the doors for the king and queen.

"King Valentin and Queen Julieta Penguin!" announced the heralds, before launching into a second trumpet fanfare.

"Welcome to Hotel Flamingo!" said Anna, curtsying.

She was amazed by how bright and orange the King and Queen Penguins' beaks were, not to mention how shiny and black their feathers. And it was impossible to miss their extravagant gowns and crowns, which were so loaded with jewels that Anna thought they

must be worth more than all of Animal Boulevard put together.

T. Bear bowed slightly, and the king and queen stepped gracefully onto the red carpet. But their gracefulness was lost amid a really loud *SQUELCH*.

Anna looked down in horror to find that the red carpet was soaked through. Bubbles had started to form on its surface. Anna bit her lip, not knowing what to do.

Despite the white sunblock on his face, T. Bear turned the color of beets. "Why is it wet?" he growled. "Why is it bubbling?"

"Which soap

powder did you use?" hissed Hilary, elbowing him in the ribs.

"The green one, of course!" he said.

"You did not," said Hilary. "This is exactly what happens when you use the red soap and add water. It'll be frothing for weeks."

T. Bear shook his head in confusion. He was certain he had used the green powder.

The royals kept smiling, knowing better than to lose their smiles in front of cameras, but with each footstep came another rude *SQUELCH*. Camera flashes burst out as they approached the hotel, and so too did a foam of white frothy bubbles.

"What a terrific little place this is," said the queen, accepting Anna's hand in her gloved wing. She lifted her feet, drawing more foam out of the carpet.

*"Ma'am" as in "jam," not "marm" as in "calm,"* thought Anna, wanting to get everything right.

"We're very pleased to have you here, ma'am," she said, grimacing.

"Very interesting red carpet!" said the king with confusion. "This frothy stuff feels top-notch whizzer on my hot feet!"

Anna didn't understand. *Perhaps royals do speak a different language?* she thought. She hurried everyone along to escape the growing mound of foam, but the royal retinue numbered at least nine penguins, not to mention the three young chicks tottering along at their feet: Boz, Tikk and Tilly. With each new pair of webbed feet

the foam on the
red carpet bubbled
higher.

The chicks loved
the carpet. After a
moment of giggles
and discussion, they launched themselves
into soapy belly slides along its length.

Ms. Chinstrap sidled next to Anna.
"We shall have words about this!" she

squawked under her breath.
"Remember, a bad review
from the king and queen
will ruin you!"

Anna had to be
professional and carry
on. "If you'd like to head
through into the lobby,"

she said politely. "We hope you'll find everything to your satisfaction."

The flamingo quartet started playing "Eine Kleine Sprat Musik," and all the hotel guests were there to witness the king and queen arrive. It was a slow, stately procession, except for the penguin chicks.

They charged through the revolving doors and hurtled off into the Piano Lounge.

Anna directed King Valentin toward the elevator. "Sir, the Royal Suite is on the fifth floor," she said. "You should find everything as you asked for. Lemmy will follow with your luggage."

"Absolutely whizz-bang," said the king cheerfully. "I hope it hasn't been too ghastly, getting things ready for our stay?"

"Oh no," said Anna, smiling. "It was nothing."

"I doubt that very much," said the queen kindly. "I'm very aware that we create a fair few problems wherever we go."

The king looked up, realizing his children had disappeared. "I say, has

anyone seen the chicks?" he asked. "They're always getting into exciting scrapes without me, those bounders!"

T. Bear appeared from the Piano Lounge with the three young penguins crawling all over him, pulling at his hat, his jacket and his nose. They were all covered in bubbles.

"I think I've found them," he said.

# 12

# The Warning

Anna was used to guests' complaints, but
Ms. Chinstrap took complaining to a
whole new level. Once the royal penguins
had settled in, the royal envoy pulled
Anna aside in the lobby.

"Up your game, Ms. Dupont," she said
with an expressionless beak. "Unless the
quality improves, the king and queen will
be leaving."

"I know. Perfection is everything," said Anna wearily.

"Exactly," said Ms. Chinstrap. She sighed and continued. "Now – and I'm not sure this is a good idea given what's just happened – the king has asked if he could host a surprise reception for the queen's birthday tomorrow evening?"

"A party?" said Anna.

The penguin nodded. "Perhaps out on the terrace? Fully exclusive, only invited guests allowed, that sort of thing."

"I'll make the arrangements right away," said Anna. "We'd be honored!"

"Good," said Ms. Chinstrap. "I will inform the king and prepare the invitations."

She waddled off into the elevator and

Anna made her way back to Lemmy at the front desk.

"Now they want a party," said Anna. "And only invited guests! We'll have to shut off the terrace."

Lemmy looked worried. He knew only too well what some of the guests would think about that. "I told you they'd have you running around in circles!" he said.

"A party?" said Mr. Camou. "How exciting! I love a chance to dress up."

Anna and Lemmy were both surprised to find the lizard leaning on the front desk. His phone was in his hand, his green fingers typing a message.

"Sorry, sir, I didn't see you there," said Anna.

"Can I help you?" asked Lemmy.

"I would like breakfast in my room tomorrow," said Mr. Camou. "Can you

arrange for a tray of fresh larvae bread to be brought at eight a.m.?"

"Certainly, sir," said Lemmy, making a note on the hotel schedule.

"It is nice to sleep in once in a while," said Mr. Camou.

"I know, sir," said Lemmy, smiling. "I also love a good long sleep."

# The Temperature Rises

The following day brought with it
news of ice cream shortages and
record-breaking temperatures. The
roads were melting, and pavements
were growing so hot that creatures
with tender paws were being advised
to stay out of the sun. But staying
indoors was also problematic,
especially if you had to work!

Anna focused solely on the surprise party. She'd crafted royal bunting to drape over the parasols, created royal fruit cocktails, and even designed a special game called "Pin the Beak on the Penguin."

"It's too hot in here, even for me!"

said Eva, carrying a tray of drinks to the terrace for some warthogs. "And I'm from Australia!"

Just then Anna heard a plate smash in the kitchen, followed by a scream. She hurtled to the restaurant. "Is everything all right?"

Madame Le Pig was spitting fury all over the kitchen. She'd thrown a giant meringue at the wall and it was slipping toward the floor. "The sea slug meringue is too chewy!" she screamed. "It is no good!"

"But why?" asked Anna.

"The heat, of course!" said Le Pig. "It is too hot in here. It is unbearable! I cannot create party food in these conditions."

"You're too hot?" said Anna, thinking kitchens were always hot. "Is the air-conditioning not working?"

"How should I know?" said Le Pig. "I AM THE CHEF!"

"Yes, I know that," said Anna.

"Then sort out this heat!" squealed Le Pig. "IT IS IMPOSSIBLE! My batters are getting battered!"

Anna hurried off, but hadn't gotten farther than the restaurant before Ms. Chinstrap found her.

"The heat is close to tropical upstairs," she said. "The young chicks are most put out. Please deal with it, or I shall be forced to approach the Glitz for alternative accommodation."

Lemmy was at the front desk, talking on the phone.

"Did you turn up the air-conditioning as I asked?" said Anna.

Lemmy nodded, covering the mouthpiece with his hand. "Of course."

"How odd," said Anna.

She went downstairs to the basement and when she opened the air-conditioning unit a sprawling nest of very important-looking wires flopped out. Most were cut, twisted and totally ruined.

"No wonder it's not working," she said. "What on earth's happened here?"

# 14

# Sabotage

Stella pulled apart the messy ball of wiring with her hooves. Detailed, fiddly work such as wiring was not her strong point, but even she could see what was wrong.

"Someone's had a real go at this," she said.

"Someone?" asked Anna.

"Oh yeah," Stella replied. "Whoever did this knew exactly what they were doing. They've cut through the wires, fusing the

system, which has blown the TCU."

"The what?" said Anna.

"The thing that controls it all," said Stella. "I'll have to order a new part. Could take weeks."

"But who would do such a thing?"

"Someone wanting to break it, I should think," replied Stella.

Anna held her head in her hands. "All our guests will leave," she said. "Or melt! No one will be able to bear the heat!"

"I could patch it myself," said Stella. "But you wouldn't be able to change the temperature. It'll be ice-cold – or super hot – all day long."

A bead of sweat rolled down Anna's forehead. "Right now," she said, "ice-cold would be very cool."

"Leave it to me," said Stella calmly.

•

With Stella's hard work the temperature in the hotel soon dropped to near freezing, which made the royal penguins very happy. They could wear their jeweled gowns once more without so much as breaking a sweat.

Anna wrapped a scarf around her neck to keep warm and called an emergency meeting. "This is sabotage," she told her team. "Someone is trying to break our hotel."

"Surely not?" said T. Bear, shivering.

"Mr. Ruffian threatened us, didn't he?" said Anna. "I thought he'd done all the damage he could do, but maybe I underestimated him?"

"I must admit, darling," said Ms. Fragranti, whose long legs were knocking together from the cold, "I wouldn't put it past him."

"He bought all the ice at the port," said Anna, "then there was the red-carpet disaster, and now the air-conditioning. What next?"

"But Mr. Ruffian's not been here at all," said Eva, her teeth chattering.

"He doesn't need to be, darling," said Ms. Fragranti. "That man has power and money. He'll have spies everywhere."

Anna gasped. "You think there's a spy here? One of our guests?"

Everyone grumbled. It was a horrible thought.

"If anyone tampers with my kitchen," said Madame Le Pig, "I shall bake them in a pie!"

"But who could it be?" said Anna. "The party is tonight and we can't have anything else go wrong. Our hotel's reputation depends on it. And no scarves tonight, no matter how cold it is in here!"

"Miss Anna," said T. Bear, puffing out his chest, "Lemmy and I will get to the bottom of this. Don't you worry."

With the meeting over everyone left the office where they found a mob of angry warthogs, meerkats and zebras waiting for them. Mrs. Bamba took on the role of leader.

"Aha!" she said, upon spotting Anna. "It is freezing in this hotel, which as we all know is perfect for penguins but not for us. And how are we supposed to swim on an iceberg? The pool is no longer fit for a wallow, let alone a swim!"

Anna felt awful. Jojo had warned her of this. Everything she'd been doing lately was for the sole benefit of the King and Queen Penguin. *Everyone is welcome at Hotel Flamingo*, she reminded herself.

"We are having problems with the air-conditioning," she said. "I'm truly sorry."

"Can't you turn it off?" asked Mrs. Bamba. "I've got icicles on my tusks – and I'm not the only one!"

"I'll see what I can do," Anna said. "For now, though, all hot drinks are on

the house. Hot chocolate, tea, coffee.
Have as much as you like."

"Thank you very much," said Mrs.
Bamba. "And the swimming pool?"

Lemmy had been
listening in to the
conversation, and
he knew full well
where a pool-sized
hole now existed in
the hotel grounds.
When you dig up
a lot of mud, you
make a big hole. "I
think I may be able
to help," he said.

# Detective Bear

T. Bear and Lemmy pawed through the reservation book at the front desk.

"Whoever is doing this must have arrived after we received the royal letter," said T. Bear.

"Well, that could be anyone from the tour bus. Warthogs? Zebras?"

"Doesn't seem likely."

"What about that lizard?"

"Let's look at this sensibly," growled T. Bear. "Whoever cut the wires in the air-conditioning must have used tools."

"Or metal teeth!" said Lemmy, remembering the flash of gold from  Ronnie Rathbone's mouth. "And she had a really heavy bag. It could have been full of tools!"

T. Bear remembered seeing Ronnie outside the hotel when the King and Queen Penguin arrived. "She was there when I was laying out the red carpet!" he said, slamming the book shut. "She could have soaked it!"

"The dirty rat!" said Lemmy.

"We just need proof," said T. Bear. "I'll have to watch her and catch her red-handed."

But when T. Bear searched the hotel from top to bottom he couldn't find her anywhere. He knew the stakes were high. If she was up to no good, it could be the end of Hotel Flamingo.

•

Late in the afternoon, the royal penguins were enjoying the exclusive use of the pool. Under Jojo's watchful eye the three chicks took turns to slide down the iceberg, while the king and queen lounged underneath parasols, reading and nibbling on seafood treats.

"Jolly lovely here, eh?" said the king.

"I knew it would be the moment I saw the pictures in *Hot Hotels* magazine," said the queen.

Ms. Chinstrap was pleased to see everything running so smoothly.

"How much longer do you think our royal guests will be out here?" Anna asked, approaching her. "We've got a lot to do to get ready for tonight."

"I shall pass on the word to His

Majesty," said Ms. Chinstrap and waddled off.

Thankfully the king was very good at finding a way to distract the penguin chicks.

"Golly gosh!" he squawked, leaping to his feet. "If I was any hotter, I think my beak would melt!"

"How awful you'd look then," said the queen with a giggle.

"Quite!" said the king, laughing. "Come on, chicklets, let's go and find some hidden treasure inside. And that goes for you too, my queen. I wouldn't want *your* beak melting out here!"

The king winked at Anna and herded his family playfully into the hotel, followed by Ms. Chinstrap.

Anna and Eva placed signs around the pool and draped the bunting from one parasol to the next. While they worked, Anna explained how she wanted everything to look.

"The flamingos will be here," she
said, pointing to a spot poolside. "Then
you'll be stationed in the Beach Hut Bar,
serving smoothies and nibbles, and I'll
walk among the crowd taking orders.

And keep a close watch on everyone.
I can't have another thing go wrong."

"Nothing will go wrong on my
watch," said Eva. "Don't you worry."

KARAOKE
FOR
DUCKS
6PM
PIANO
LOUNGE

# Surprises for All

T. Bear returned sad-faced and empty-handed to the lobby.

"Any luck?" asked Anna.

"Sorry, miss. But I'll get the culprit, I promise."

Ms. Chinstrap stepped out of the elevator, tipping Squeak the elevator operator handsomely. The quiet and retiring old mouse's eyes lit up at the money in his paw.

"Everything ready?" asked Ms. Chinstrap. "The first guests will arrive soon, and the king is very excited. I wouldn't want to let him down."

"Come and see the terrace," said Anna. "I think you'll be happy."

She asked Lemmy to watch the front desk and told T. Bear to usher the guests through to the party. He growled dutifully, then took his place on the front door.

One by one the VIPs arrived, and
T. Bear showed them out onto the
terrace, announcing their names and
hoping he was saying them right. There
were armadillos in bow ties, rhinos in ball
gowns, storks in skirts, and even a vampire
bat in her finest evening attire.

The golden setting sun lit up the
terrace. It looked spectacular, with orange
light shimmering off the iceberg, sending
sparkles out onto the guests.

As time rolled on whispers drifted around the growing crowd that the king and queen were due to arrive.

The guests fell silent as T. Bear walked

onto the terrace with a stony face. "Mr. Ronald Ruffian," he growled.

"What's he doing here?" said Anna, racing to Ms. Chinstrap.

"He's a friend of the queen," she said curtly.

The lion swaggered in as if he owned the place, a pompous smile on his face. He was followed by a group of his own staff pulling a huge cart topped with a towering ice sculpture of the King and Queen Penguin. They parked it in the middle of the terrace for everyone to see.

"What's he up to?" said Eva.

"He's trying to show us up," said Anna. "What a cheek!"

But before Anna could give him a piece of her mind, a trumpet fanfare erupted.

"Their Royal Majesties, King Valentin and Queen Julieta Penguin!" announced T. Bear.

The two royal penguins waddled into view dressed in splendid evening dress, followed by their three young chicks. Queen Julieta's face lit up at the sight of everyone.

"A surprise party?!" she cried, jumping into the air with happiness.

"Good evening," said the king, "and thank you for joining us on this absolute whizz-popper of an occasion. Please join me in a toast: to my sweet diddums, the queen!"

Everyone raised their glasses and clinked them together before a chorus of "hurrahs" shook the terrace. As the cheers turned to chatter, Ms. Fragranti's string quartet burst into life, directed by the flamboyant flamingo herself. But they only managed four notes before the strings on the instruments twinged, twanged and snapped.

The music fell silent. All eyes were on Ms. Fragranti, and for all the wrong reasons.

"Oh no," said Anna. "What now?"

# 17

# Party Poopers

"It must have been the heat!" explained Ms. Fragranti to Anna as her flamingos hurriedly tried to restring their instruments. "I will sing a verse or two until we're ready again."

Ms. Fragranti belted out an old show tune as Anna took a closer look at the broken strings. There were tiny little cuts along their lengths. "Someone's been at work here again," she said.

The queen caught sight of Anna and held up her wing to get her attention. "Ms. Dupont, thank you so much for all this!" she cried. "And the ice sculpture is PERFECT!"

Anna cringed. It was her worst nightmare come true. And to make things even worse Mr. Ruffian was gloating at her from behind the queen.

"I think you'll find that was my gift, Your Majesty," he said, leaning forward.

"Ronald!" declared the queen. "So wonderful to see you here."

"I do like visiting other hotels, ma'am," he replied, "though the Glitz really is the best at throwing parties."

Anna had never felt more angry. "I

think we should let the guests decide that," she said, smiling through gritted teeth. She made her apologies for leaving, and then strode away into the hotel.

A crowd of noisy monkeys had gathered in the lobby to watch the royal  party through the windows. The warthogs were grumbling to T. Bear about not being invited, while the hoglets ran free, unwatched.

"Someone tampered with the instruments," said Anna to T. Bear, taking deep breaths to calm herself.

"I've let you down," said T. Bear, looking at his paws. "I thought I knew who'd been up to no good, but I haven't been able to find her."

"Her?" said Anna.

"The rat, Ms. Rathbone," he said.

"Ronnie? But she seemed so nice!" said Anna.

"All of the clues lead to her," said T. Bear. "We knew that it had to be someone who arrived after that letter. The rat fits the bill perfectly."

Madame Le Pig appeared, pushing a cart of platters loaded with squid scones and sea slug meringues.

"Absolute perfection!" said Anna. "Shall we take them outside?"

"Of course! Before they freeze in this icebox of an hotel!" snorted Le Pig.

"Thank you, chef," said Anna, and she and T. Bear pushed the cart out to the terrace.

"Squid scones, ma'am?" T. Bear asked the queen, moving the cart forward with gusto.

At that very moment the cart wobbled uncontrollably. One leg fell apart, and everything tipped sideways. A dozen freshly baked squid scones – dripping in seaweed jam and gloopy clotted cream – went flying through the air. They splattered at full force onto the queen.

The crowd gasped in horror.

# 18

# Pointing the Finger

"Good gracious!" squawked the queen as seaweed jam dripped down her face.

Anna raced to help. When she saw the mess she wanted to cry.

"What happened?!" she asked.

"That bear just threw scones over the queen!" spat Ms. Chinstrap. She began wiping jam off the queen's face with her wing tip.

"It was the cart!" said T. Bear, picking up a screw.

"Don't worry!" said Mr. Ruffian, helping the queen. He passed her his pocket handkerchief. "We have brought our own squid scones. We have this covered."

He called out to his staff, and within seconds they were wheeling out cartloads of scones.

"Honestly, ma'am," he said, "small hotels like this one just aren't cut out for hosting guests such as yourself. These won't fall over on you."

"But someone must have fiddled with the cart!" said T. Bear.

"Don't be so ridiculous," said Mr. Ruffian. "It's badly made, just like everything else at Hotel Flamingo."

Anna picked up the wheel and more screws and examined them. "He's not lying. Someone's unscrewed them!"

The terrace door slammed and the crowd gasped. Madame Le Pig had marched outside with Lemmy trying to pull her back.

"WHAT IS THE MEANING OF THIS!" she cried, scooping up a handful of the scones that had been delivered from the Glitz. "I will not have this rubbish served to the queen!" spat Le Pig. "Who brought this horrid food into my hotel?"

"I did," said Mr. Ruffian, who started laughing. "You are a funny and rather sad excuse for a chef."

Madame Le Pig rolled up her sleeves in anger, then removed her chef's hat and threw it to the floor. "I will fight you here and now!" she exclaimed, scraping her trotters across the floor like a raging bull.

"STOP THIS NOW!" Anna cried, blocking the path between Mr. Ruffian and the chef. "You are embarrassing all of us, Madame Le Pig."

The queen took the king's wing. "This has taken a rather sour turn," she said. "I think we should maybe retire to our suite."

"No! Please! No!" said Anna. "King Valentin and Queen Julieta, ever since

153

you canceled your reservation at the Glitz Mr. Ruffian has been trying to ruin everything for us."

"Goodness, Ms. Dupont," said the queen. "Mr. Ruffian is a very good friend of ours. Where is your proof?"

"He brought his hotel food to our party!" said Anna. "Who does that?"

"I know your food is not up to royal standards," said Mr. Ruffian.

Madame Le Pig could stand it no more. She charged at the lion, hitting him square in the chest with her snout and knocking him to the floor.

Squeals and gasps of horror echoed around the terrace.

"Wowsers! What a jolly smasher of an uppercut!" said the king.

The queen was appalled. "No more of this!" she pleaded.

T. Bear snatched Madame Le Pig up into the air before she could charge again. The pig dangled helplessly and furiously as Mr. Ruffian picked up his wallet and keys. The chef had packed such a wallop that all the lion's belongings had flown across the floor.

"Stop this now!" ordered Anna.

Mr. Ruffian laughed and brushed himself down. Madame Le Pig snorted in disgust.

"I'll put you out of business for this," he growled.

"What more could you do?" said Anna. "You've already ruined everything!"

"A very *unlikely* story," said Mr.

Ruffian. "The king and queen really ought to transfer their belongings to the Glitz. This is quite out of order."

"I agree," said Ms. Chinstrap. "We will settle our bill and leave. I've had enough of this."

"As have I," said the king sadly. "And this was such a jolly wobbler of a hotel."

"Please don't leave," pleaded Anna. "This wasn't our fault!"

"I'm sorry, Ms. Dupont," said the queen. "I can see you've tried very hard to make us welcome, but your hotel is sadly not fit for a king or queen."

"Quite right," said Mr. Ruffian. "Collect up their things, Ms. Chinstrap. I shall arrange everything else."

Ms. Chinstrap sniffed and looked to Anna. "Front desk in five minutes," she said, before leaving the terrace. Mr. Ruffian followed, gloating as only he could.

Anna slumped to the floor in tears as the party guests slowly drifted away. "We're finished," she said, crestfallen.

"No," said T. Bear, stamping. "There

158

has to be something we can do!"

Lemmy walked toward them. "We've got one last throw of the dice," he said. "I really don't want to do this, but I think I have to."

# 19

# A Big Mistake

"Please give us one chance to explain," said Anna, her teeth chattering as she stood in the freezing-cold lobby. "One chance."

"You'd better have the perfect excuse," said Ms. Chinstrap. "I want facts. Cold hard facts and nothing less."

The elevator bell chimed, the doors opened and Lemmy appeared, carrying a large, heavy bag. He threw it down at Ms. Chinstrap's feet. "I took this from Ronnie Rathbone's room," he said. "She's been sabotaging everything. What's inside will prove it!"

Anna rallied herself and unzipped it. A pile of clothes and trinkets, and a lifetime's worth of keepsakes rolled out. Lemmy stared at them in surprise.

"What has this to do with anything?" said Ms. Chinstrap, pushing her glasses up her beak.

"It wasn't her," said Lemmy, realizing he'd made a terrible mistake.

"Then who was it?" said Anna.

"Oh, this is too much," said Ms. Chinstrap. "Goodbye, Ms. Dupont. I do not hope to see you again."

The tension was broken by Eva walking into the lobby carrying a phone. "Is this anyone's?" she asked, passing it to Anna. "I found it on the terrace."

The phone was gold plated and looked very expensive. *There is only one creature who would own a phone like that,* thought Anna.

As she flipped it over in her hand
it started to ring. She immediately
recognized the caller's name on the display.

"I don't believe it," said Anna.

"What now?" said Ms. Chinstrap,
losing her patience.

Anna looked at T. Bear. "You suspected
the wrong guest!"

Anna worked through everything in
her mind. "It's crystal clear to me now,"
she said. "The creature causing us all
these problems just called this phone. And
I am pretty sure I know who owns it."

"Don't tease us," said T. Bear. "Who is
it?"

Suddenly Ronnie Rathbone came
through the front door. She looked down
and saw her belongings lying everywhere.

"What do you think you're doing?" she said sharply.

"I'm so, so sorry," said Anna, "but please hear us out. I can make all of this right."

"You'd better have a good explanation, kid," said Ronnie.

Anna was set to explain everything when the elevator doors chimed, and the King and Queen Penguin appeared, followed by Mr. Ruffian and their three chicks. The young penguins looked desperately sad to be leaving.

"We're ready," said the king to Ms. Chinstrap.

"And I see you've found my phone," said Mr. Ruffian, attempting to snatch it out of Anna's hand.

Anna was too quick for the lion,

whipping the phone behind her back. "Good grief," she said. "So it really *was* you!"

Ms. Chinstrap lowered her glasses. "What is going on?" she ordered.

Anna redialed the number that had just called Mr. Ruffian's phone. "Listen," she said, raising her hand.

They waited in silence for a few seconds, before hearing another phone ringing in the Piano Lounge. The ringing quickly stopped.

"Come with me," said Anna.

"I'm not taking part in this charade!" said Mr. Ruffian. "Give me my phone back."

But Anna wouldn't. She marched into the Piano Lounge, followed by everyone,

and found the room occupied only by
warthogs. They were playing board
games and chuckling to themselves.

"Can you see anything?" asked Anna.

"Yes!" said Ms. Chinstrap angrily. "Warthogs."

"No, no. Look at the curtains," said Anna, smiling. "The game's up, Mr. Camou."

# 20

## Caught in the Act

The patterned curtains shimmered, then started to move, and as if by magic Mr. Camou suddenly became visible. He looked incredibly awkward, as he was completely nude, except for his mobile phone and a screwdriver.

The King Penguin covered his eyes to preserve his dignity, while T. Bear rushed to get a tablecloth from the restaurant.

He wrapped this around Mr. Camou, then took hold of his wrist with a very strong paw. "I thought he was just a lizard," explained Anna, "but Mr. Camou is much more than that. He is a chameleon. He can change his skin color to match his surroundings and pretty much become invisible."

"That's like magic!" said Lemmy.

"Isn't it?" said Anna. "And he's also a friend of Mr. Ruffian. They've planned all of this together." She then described all the problems they'd faced during the royal stay.

"Is this true, Ronald?" asked the queen quietly.

"This is all nonsense!" said the lion. "I would never embarrass you like this."

"Did you do these things?" Ms. Chinstrap asked the lizard. "Did Mr. Ruffian have a hand in it?"

Mr. Camou's skin turned a shade of custard yellow. "Espionage is what I am good at, and Mr. Ruffian pays so well," he said. "As my beautiful skin allows me to hide in plain sight I can do all kinds of things without anyone noticing."

"You changed the labels on the carpet cleaner!" said T. Bear. "So I didn't get it wrong!"

"No, you didn't," said Mr. Camou shamefully. His whole body turned bright pink with embarrassment.

"I will sue this horrible hotel for all it has!" roared Mr. Ruffian. "These are lies! All lies. It is a setup!"

"I'm not so sure," said the queen.

Mr. Ruffian bumped Lemmy out of the way and stormed out of the hotel.

"Wait for me!" cried Mr. Camou, scuttling after him.

He left everyone in a stunned silence.

"I hope that's the last we see of them!" said Anna.

"How would we ever know?" said the king, laughing. "What an absolute cad!"

"I think we owe you a very big apology," said the queen. "I didn't think Ronald would mind us changing our plans to stay at Hotel Flamingo instead of the Glitz. How wrong I was."

Anna turned to Ronnie, who was enjoying the show. "Ms. Rathbone," said Anna, "I'm truly sorry we suspected you. How can we make it up to you?"

Ronnie flashed her gold teeth with a smile.

"You're not unusual for thinking a rat's up to no good," she said. "I've had worse."

"That doesn't make it OK, Ms. Rathbone," said Anna. "We won't be charging you for your stay."

"Does this mean we're staying too?" asked one of the penguin chicks.

"Yes, my cheeky chicklet. I think it does," said the king. "And that's the best whizz-popping news I've heard all week!"

The three chicks leapt onto T. Bear and cheered.

"I'm pleased too," said the queen, smiling. "I do love this little hotel. And Madame Le Pig's squid scones truly were the best I've ever tasted, even if I did have to lick them off my gown."

T. Bear laughed a very deep laugh.

"I wonder," said the king, taking Anna to one side, "would you mind if we got the party started again? Such a crashing bore to miss out on a good dance!"

"There is nothing I would like more!" said Anna. "But Hotel Flamingo is open to all guests – warthogs, penguins and *especially* rats. This time, everyone's invited."

"What a jolly good idea," replied the king. "Now where are those flamingos? They play a mighty good tune."

# 21

# Muddy End

Without Mr. Camou to cause trouble the
hotel was soon running smoothly again
as was the air-conditioning. The King
and Queen Penguin had taken to eating
their meals with the other guests and their
chicks had made firm friends with Mrs.
Bamba's young hoglets.

Anna was thrilled to see every creature
getting along. Her dream of making Hotel

Flamingo the most welcoming hotel on Animal Boulevard was coming true. Even the royal envoy was enjoying herself.

"I must say," said Ms. Chinstrap, while relaxing on the terrace, "I think I can now see the appeal of your hotel."

"Thank you," said Anna proudly.

"Perhaps perfection doesn't always rest in things being perfectly tidy, or perfectly clean, or perfectly presented," she said.

"Perhaps perfection is also about a feeling of happiness."

Anna watched the three penguin chicks race past, followed by the hoglets. They bundled through a hedgerow, running out of sight, before making a

huge splash. Dollops of mud flew through the air, hitting Anna in the face.

Anna went to investigate. Where once there had been a huge flower bed behind